DOUBLE NEGATIVE

by
Charlotte Fullerton

SCHOLASTIC INC.

NEW YORK TORONTO LONDON AUCKLAND
SYDNEY MEXICO CITY NEW DELHI HONG KONG

No part of this work may be reproduced in whole or in part, or stored in a retrieval system, or transmitted in any form or by any means, electronic, mechanical, photocopying, recording, or otherwise, without written permission of the publisher. For information regarding permission, write to Scholastic Inc., Attention: Permissions Department, 557 Broadway, New York, NY 10012.

4239 8122 X10

ISBN: 978-0-545-17716-0

Cartoon Network, the logo, BEN 10 ALIEN FORCE and all related characters and elements are trademarks of and © 2010 Cartoon Network.

SCHOLASTIC and associated logos are trademarks and/or registered trademarks of Scholastic Inc.

12 11 10 9 8 7 6 5 4 3 2 1   10 11 12 13 14/0   40

Designed by Rick DeMonico
Printed in the U.S.A.
First printing, January 2010

And the cube root of 1,331 is 11, which is, of course," he paused dramatically for effect, "a prime number."

With a flourish, fifteen-year-old Ben Tennyson finished scribbling in his physics notebook, then leaned back and casually rested one sneakered foot on the edge of the kitchen table. Hanging behind him on his chair, brushing the floor as he tipped back, was Ben's signature long-sleeved green jacket with its white racing stripes and the number "10" prominently emblazoned in black and white.

Sitting next to him in his family's kitchen was Ben's bright, pretty girlfriend, Julie Yamamoto. She dropped her pencil on the floor in absolute shock. "Wow, Ben. You sure have been studying! I'm impressed. Usually I'm the one who has to explain science and math stuff to you."

"Aw, it's really nothing," countered Ben modestly, leaning in to take a loud slurp from the straw of the Mr. Smoothy takeout cup on the table in front of him. Suddenly, his expression turned sour and his green eyes bulged as he fought to choke the mouthful down. "Ugh! What flavor is this thing? It tastes like feet!"

Julie rummaged through her school backpack and pulled out the receipt to double-check her order. "Peanut butter seaweed, one of your favorites. Just like you always ask me to pick up before we do our homework together," she said, eyeing Ben curiously.

"Right. How silly of me. It's delicious. My favorite. Yum." Ben wrenched his grimace into a smile and noisily drank the rest. "I don't know what I was thinking."

"You just have your mind on your homework, Ben. Which I have to admit is kind of nice for a change," Julie said.

With a lull in the alien activity in Bellwood and the galaxy not needing too much saving recently, Julie was grateful that Ben was finally getting a chance to lead the life of a normal teenager, at least for a little while.

The chunky green-and-black watch strapped onto his left wrist was a constant reminder of Ben's heroic destiny. But the Omnitrix hadn't needed to be used in—wait, how long had it been since Ben had transformed into one of his alien creatures, anyway?

"I'll tell you what, Ben, you've obviously been studying hard lately," Julie said, closing her book. "You've got this physics stuff down. I say it's time for a Burger Shack break."

"A break, yes, okay, good," Ben agreed eagerly. He reached back for his jacket and bounced up from his seat, nearly knocking his chair over. "Whoa!"

"Careful." Julie grabbed the chair to keep it from falling.

"One of the many perils of being a teenager. I'm still not used to this body," muttered Ben in irritation. Then he added with a good-natured chuckle, "I mean, it's embarrassing being such a klutz sometimes, but my parents say everybody goes through it. It's all part of growing up."

"They're right," Julie agreed, packing up her schoolbooks and heading through the living room toward the front door. "Don't worry about it. You're only human, after all."

Her comment made Ben smile. As they passed a bookshelf behind the couch cluttered with family keepsakes, a particular framed photo caught Ben's eye—a picture of himself and his cousin Gwen when they were both ten years old. They were posing arm in arm with their Grandpa Max. Julie spoke up, certain she knew what Ben was going to say, what he always said whenever he looked at that photo: "Best summer of your life, huh?" She elbowed him playfully.

But Ben just stared back at her blankly.

"Hello? The summer you found the Omnitrix?" Was he kidding her? Julie didn't always get Ben's sense of humor.

"Yes, of course, the Omnitrix." Ben's green eyes lit up. "The summer that changed my life. Right, of course, *that* summer. Good times, good times."

"All this studying must be frying your brain, Ben," kidded Julie, tousling his brown hair. "We'd better hurry and get some food into you, mister." She playfully pushed him out the front door of the house. "Chili fries on me!"

At the mention of chili fries, Ben perked up. "Chili-*cheese* fries? Now *that's* my favorite! One of the best things on Earth!"

The one and only Burger Shack location in Bellwood was doing a bustling suppertime business as usual, especially with the high school crowd. Teenagers sat both at and on the handful of concrete tables outside, while others waited in the long line at the counter inside to order.

One car in the parking lot stood out from all the others. It was a bright green, 1970s muscle car with two thick black racing stripes. It was the kind of collectible car that had been lovingly restored by its owner to its factory condition and then some.

As a middle-aged customer precariously maneuvered his family's takeout tray of burgers and fries into his own car, he leaned on the green car for a split second to steady himself. At this, a young man's voice called out harshly from across the parking lot: "Not cool, dude! Step away from my ride!"

Kevin Levin, Ben's sixteen-year-old former enemy, now loyal ally—though he'd be loath to admit they were friends—slouched back against one of the outdoor tables, outstretched legs crossed, never taking an eye off his most prized possession. It was his second car, actually. The first one had been destroyed while Kevin was saving the Earth from invasion by hostile alien beings called the HighBreed. Kevin's beloved set of wheels was a casualty of that war. But once the dust had settled, he'd managed to score another classic car just like it at the auto show, and ever since, he'd been spending every waking moment tricking out his new baby.

"Relax, Kevin, will you?" His girlfriend, Gwen, smiled at him from across the table, where she'd been engaged in an intense whispered discussion with Julie. "It's not like your car—excuse me, your 'ride,'" Gwen made sarcastic air quotes as she spoke, "can't handle a little scratch with all the alien tech modifications you've already made to it."

"I don't like people touching my car," groused Kevin. "And you know what, Gwen? If I ever *didn't* complain about it, you'd know something was wrong with me."

"That's exactly the kind of thing I'm talking about!" Julie segued back to the hushed conversation she'd been having with Gwen. She glanced over her shoulder to be absolutely sure Ben couldn't hear. He was at the front of the line inside the Burger Shack, finally getting his turn to order. He smiled goofily and waved enthusiastically at his friends through the big plate-glass window.

"Something about Ben lately seems, I don't know, *different*," confided Julie. "Have you two noticed anything weird? Or am I just imagining it?"

"Weird like what?" Gwen asked. "Tentacles growing out of his head?"

"Weird like studying really hard, especially math and science, and doing extremely well on his physics homework, and uh—" Julie ceased ticking off the items on her fingers when she realized how ridiculous she sounded.

"Studying? Homework? Oh, yeah, that's insane behavior all right." Kevin smirked. "We'd better put a stop to it right away."

"Okay, okay. I know it doesn't sound like anything," Julie said, a little embarrassed, "but it's not just that he's suddenly doing amazingly well in science. It's all kinds of little things here and there. I can't explain it. But I'm telling you guys, something about him seems a little . . . off."

"I wouldn't worry too much about it, Julie," Gwen offered reassuringly. "Sometimes boys just *are* a little off."

"Maybe he's trying to break up with you and just can't think of how to tell you," mused Kevin. Gwen silenced him with a quick swat. "Ow! Hey! I'm just saying. It happens."

"What happens?" Ben was suddenly standing right behind Julie and Gwen, holding a tray overloaded with burgers and massive amounts of chili-cheese fries.

"Nothing!" Julie and Gwen said in unison.

"Mind if I dig in? It feels like I haven't had chili-cheese fries in forever." Ben sat down between Julie and Gwen. Without waiting for his friends to answer, he started chowing down the entire tray of chili-cheese fries, barely pausing between gulps. The girls looked at each other, disgusted. Ben didn't even seem to mind there was chili dripping from his chin.

"Save some for us, Tennyson," noted Kevin dryly.

Gwen's right, thought Julie. *Boys just are weird sometimes.*

That night, Ben lay in his bed, wide awake and staring at the ceiling. He hadn't slept a wink. His stomach rumbled, probably from all those chili-cheese fries he'd scarfed down earlier. He'd better learn to pace himself in the future.

While Mr. and Mrs. Tennyson slept soundly in the other room, Ben watched as the digital clock on his nightstand blinked from "1:59" to "2:00." Then he carefully crept out of bed and got dressed.

In downtown Bellwood, all was quiet and still under the low light of the crescent moon. The streetlight hanging in the intersection at the end of the block cast an eerie red glow over the silhouette of a figure slowly making his way down a row of darkened storefronts. The figure stepped out of the shadows and approached the door of a rickety, old-fashioned plumbing supply shop. It was Ben.

Ben's eyes moved toward the broken panel of doorbells on the wall. There was a handwritten sign taped over it: BUZZER BROKEN. PLEASE KNOCK. Ben made a fist and punched the beat-up panel, knocking it free. The rusty placard swung open, revealing the glistening console of a high-tech security clearance system hidden behind it. Its infrared beam was trained squarely on Ben.

"Ben Tennyson," recited Ben evenly as the beam scanned his cells for verification.

"DNA identified," a computerized voice intoned. "Ben Tennyson. Access granted."

A secret steel door beside the plumbing supply company's ramshackle entrance slid open, and Ben silently slipped inside. With a hum, the floor under his feet began to lower as the portal whizzed closed behind him and bolted itself securely with an intimidating series of clangs and clicks. Whatever this place was, Ben was now locked in, and everyone else in the world was locked out.

Deep within the fortified basement below, the security elevator doors whooshed open. Ben grinned widely as he stepped out into the top secret, seldom-used, Bellwood headquarters of the Plumbers.

These kind of Plumbers didn't have anything to do with water pipes. No, this organization of Plumbers was a classified, elite, intergalactic police force of highly trained officers sworn to serve and protect the galaxy from all hostile uprisings and—in the case of the Plumbers stationed on this planet—to monitor the Earth for alien activity. Ben and Gwen's very own Grandpa Max was one of its veteran members.

So much the stranger, then, that Max's grandson, Ben Tennyson, wielder of the Omnitrix, hero of the universe, would need to break into this highly fortified Plumber HQ.

"Excellent security," Ben snickered as he made a bee-line for the database of confidential intelligence gathered by Plumbers throughout the galaxy. Ben's fingerprint identification allowed him full access to the Plumbers' computer system. As he used the touchpad to scroll through the file names, a familiar green and black hour-glass symbol winked onto the screen. He scrolled back. "That's it!" He had found the Plumbers' most highly classified intel: Everything you ever wanted to know about the Omnitrix but were afraid to ask! Ben's green eyes lit up with greed. "Yes! It's all here!"

But before Ben could open the onscreen file, the dark room was suddenly flooded with light. Ben shielded his eyes and spun around, startled. "Who? Where? What?"

"Us. Here. To kick your butt, *Ben*." Kevin stepped out from behind some machinery, fists clenched, ready for a fight.

"Or should we say, Albedo." Gwen appeared from behind a corner on the other side of Ben, magenta circles of manna energy already crackling at her fingertips.

"How did you two get in here?" sputtered Ben.

Gwen and Kevin casually held up their official Plumbers' badges.

Ben suddenly started violently as if he were waking up from a nightmare. He rubbed his eyes, shook his head, and looked at his friends, melodramatically confused. "Where am I? I must have been sleepwalking."

"Save it, you imposter," spat Kevin. "We're wise to you."

Gwen held up her energized fists threateningly. "Julie didn't meet you the first time you were around, Albedo, so of course she had no idea what to make of Ben acting strangely. But as soon as she told us, we immediately suspected Ben wasn't himself. He was you!"

Before Albedo-Ben could move, Gwen fired energy beams at him, scanning for his life force, beyond his DNA—which, thanks to Albedo's old, malfunctioning, knockoff Omnitrix, was absolutely identical to Ben's DNA. A moment later, his true identity was revealed. As Albedo-Ben struggled futilely in the grip of Gwen's powerful manna field, his brown hair washed out into a shocking white, and the green of his eyes and his jacket flickered into their opposite color, red. Ben's evil duplicate, Albedo, also known as Negative Ben, stood before them in all his glory!

"I guess the jig is, as they say, up," Albedo said calmly, straightening his red jacket and running his fingers through his bleached hair to smooth it down. "Pity so soon. I was so looking forward to more chili-cheese fries."

"You dyed your hair, you wore one of Ben's jackets. How did you turn your eyes green?" Kevin insisted.

"What, you think I'm smart enough to make my own Omnitrix, but that I can't figure out how to put in colored contact lenses? Gah. Humans!" Albedo shook his head in disgust.

"Never mind that," shouted Gwen, lassoing Albedo in a thin stream of manna energy, pinning his arms to his sides. She strode right up to his smirking face to demand, "How long have you been here in Bellwood living Ben's life? And where is the real Ben Tennyson?"

CHAPTER TWO

At that very moment, the real Ben Tennyson was being roughly thrown into a dank, windowless prison cell by a hulking robotic monstrosity called a Techadon. As his head hit the floor, Ben glimpsed the thick metal cell door latch behind him. With that, his jailer was gone.

Identifying his assailants as Techadons, however, provided Ben not a clue to his captor's true identity. Ben and his friends had fought Techadons before, but as Kevin had explained at the time, these kinds of mechanical drones were a dime a dozen. Techadons weren't the lackeys of any particular villain, they were mass-produced. Bad guys bought them in bulk! So not only could these Techadons be working for anybody in the entire galaxy, they could have imprisoned Ben anywhere in the universe!

Ben squinted painfully, trying to get his bearings in the darkness. "I wonder where I am? This doesn't look like Incarcecon, but it's been a long time since I've been there," Ben thought out loud, taking in what little he could of his surroundings. Five years ago, during the adventure in which he first learned the secret of the Omnitrix, Ben had been taken to a prison planet called Incarcecon. But that place was slick and techy. This was more like an old-fashioned, underground dungeon.

"The Forever Knights, maybe? Man, if those jokers are behind this, are they going to be sorry when I get out of here!" Ben punched his right fist angrily into his left, then winced as his knuckles knocked into cold, hard metal.

Ben had tried to fight back earlier, but something was very wrong. He groggily struggled to his feet now. His left arm seemed to weigh a ton, causing him to stagger sideways and drop to his knees. He felt in the darkness for the Omnitrix on his left wrist, and slammed the area repeatedly so he could transform into something— *anything*—and bust his way out of here. But a strange, bulky object was locked around his entire elbow, forearm, and hand like a cast, blocking his access to his watch.

This wasn't just any watch. It didn't even keep the correct time. No, the Omnitrix was simply the most powerful invention in the universe. Devised by the tiny but brilliant, bug-eyed scientist, Azmuth of the Galvan, the Omnitrix used DNA sampling technology to allow its wearer access to a database of, in theory, millions of sentient life forms. Not just access to learn about them — access to actually become them! If it ever fell into the wrong hands, the universe would be doomed.

Some might say that it actually *did* fall into the wrong hands when ten-year-old Ben stumbled on the Omnitrix in the woods over summer vacation. The imperiled Omnitrix had been sent to Earth in search of the greatest Plumber in the galaxy: Max Tennyson, Ben and Gwen's grandfather. Ben found the watch first, and his own DNA was so close on the spectrum to its intended recipient that the Omnitrix latched onto Ben instead of Max.

If only Ben could use it now. The Omnitrix was Azmuth's greatest creation. It had powers and properties the Galvan scientist hadn't even begun to share with Ben yet. But Azmuth had said he would in time. When Ben was ready. Maybe. If Azmuth felt like it.

"Wait just a second here . . ." Ben grew irritated as he remembered his mentor's recent grave disappointment in him for trying, with Kevin's help, to hack the Omnitrix. He had accidentally released a handful of its inhabitants — Spidermonkey, Goop, and ChromaStone — out into the world. At least he had managed to get them back. Most of them, anyway. How long was Azmuth going to hold that accident with ChromaStone against him?

"This better not be some kind of test, Azmuth!" shouted Ben. He was in no mood for games, and he didn't always understand the Galvan's sense of humor.

Ben sat down on the floor and pushed at the heavy device on his arm with both feet, trying to slide it off. He clawed at the unwieldy gadget over his arm until it gave him a painful shock. "Ouch!"

It wasn't going to budge. *Like the Omnitrix*, thought Ben grimly to himself.

Short of ripping his arm off, neither of these devices would be leaving his person anytime soon. This was going to be a problem. Without access to the Omnitrix, he was powerless. He was just plain old Ben Tennyson.

Sitting on the floor by himself in the darkness, trying to clear his head and formulate a plan, Ben slowly became aware of low murmuring in the shadows all around him. He wasn't alone! He leapt to his feet as quickly as the weighty device latched onto his arm would allow him and prepared to defend himself against the as-yet-unseen beings that seemed to be closing in on him.

By now, Ben's eyes had adjusted to the lack of light, and he was able to make out shapes moving toward him from the corners of the room. Large shapes! Several hulking figures emerged from the darkness. They seemed to be everywhere!

Ben bolted to his left and ran directly into a huge, slimy, snail creature that smelled like Swampfire on a good day. Oh, how Ben wished he could turn into Swampfire right now!

He dodged to his right and came face to chest with a crimson Tetramand not unlike Ben's own old alien form Four Arms. This grizzled prison inmate was missing one of his four arms, and Ben didn't particularly want to find out how he'd lost it.

Ben held his own heavy left arm to his belly and tucked and rolled away, this time right into a Vulpimancer, an amphibious creature with webbed feet and bulbous eyeballs on top of its arched head. It was similar to one of Ben's old transformations, WildMutt.

There were too many of them, and they had Ben surrounded! There was nowhere for him to run, and without being able to get at the Omnitrix, Ben had no way to effectively defend himself.

In the darkness of the dungeon, this collection of snarling, drooling alien creatures of many different intimidating shapes and sizes closed in on the helpless human in their midst!

CHAPTER THREE

Back on Earth, inside the Plumbers' hideout in Bellwood, Albedo-Ben teased his own captors. "'Where is the real Ben Tennyson?'" he said mockingly, repeating Gwen's words. "Wouldn't you like to know!"

"Uh, yeah, we would." Kevin rushed forward, transforming one of his hands into a giant anvil and threatening Albedo with it. "So spill."

"And what on Earth makes you think I would ever do such a thing?" Albedo asked innocently.

"Because we know that jerry-rigged duplicate Omnitrix you're wearing doesn't really work," Gwen said, releasing Albedo from her manna energy coils.

"We do?" asked Kevin incredulously. "I mean, yeah, we do!" he added emphatically.

"You can't possibly know that," sputtered a flustered Albedo.

Gwen paced in front of Albedo like a lawyer cross-examining a witness. "You've been in Bellwood for how long? And you haven't transformed once. Never mind trying to keep up appearances as Ben by pretending to do something heroic. You haven't even tried to do anything, well, you know, *evil* with your amazing powers. Including attacking us a minute ago. Because you haven't got any powers. Obviously." Gwen crossed her arms with smug satisfaction.

"So instead," Kevin surmised, clicking through the classified computer files Albedo had been browsing, "you used your identity as Ben to break into this Plumber HQ to look up info on the Omnitrix so you could finally fix yours."

Albedo's Omnitrix was indeed broken. And he hadn't always looked like an exact negative of Ben. Albedo wasn't originally a human at all. Once, he was a tiny, gray, bug-eyed Galvan, the same species as Azmuth, the creator of the Omnitrix. But he had more in common with Azmuth than that. He had been one of Azmuth's most trusted laboratory assistants.

Unfortunately for Albedo, he'd been overcome with greed while working in the lab on Galvan Prime. He'd attempted to forge his own, substandard Omnitrix and keep all its power for himself. But his knockoff Omnitrix didn't operate correctly. It trapped Albedo in the form of both Omnitrixes' default DNA setting: the human wearer of the one true Omnitrix, Ben Tennyson.

Ever since then, Albedo had been desperate to get back to his normal Galvan form. This smelly, sweaty, hairy, pimply, teenaged human body had been irritating him to no end. The craving for chili-cheese fries alone was unbearable! The first time Albedo had shown up in Bellwood, he'd been looking to use Ben's Omnitrix to release him from his prison inside Ben's human body. He and Ben had fought to a draw, and their two Omnitrixes had locked. The feedback of negative energy had altered Albedo's coloring, making it the opposite of Ben's.

Still worse for Albedo, Azmuth had appeared and had punished his traitorous former assistant by removing the watch-face control from the lesser, duplicate Omnitrix. Now Albedo was trapped as Ben's mirror image forever. For Albedo, this was a fate worse than death.

"And you're going right back to Azmuth's lockup now if you don't tell us where Ben is," Gwen said sternly, taking a step toward Albedo.

"Maybe so, maybe so," Negative Ben quipped, "but you'll have to catch me first!"

He may not have had a working Omnitrix on his wrist, but Albedo knew this Plumbers' hideout would be crawling with alien tech weaponry. Most Earth technology was classified as Level 2. Albedo, like Ben, was a scrappy fighter and was able to improvise with whatever was at hand. He grabbed a Level 5 blaster off the wall and sprayed the room with laser fire!

"Look out, Kevin!" Gwen shouted. With a wave of her hand, she created a curved shield of manna energy to take the impact of the blasts.

"I got this!" Kevin shouted back, peeling off the ID mask that made him appear human. Underneath was his actual, grossly mutated form—the result of a recent, terrible accident that had occurred when he and Ben had tried to hack the Omnitrix. Now half of Kevin's head, including his hair, was made out of crystal material, while the other half was concrete. A portion of his body appeared to be made out of metal, while his legs were formed from some unidentifiable alien compound.

Ever since his life-changing accident, Kevin had lost his old powers of matter absorption, but he was able to alter his fists into enormous boulders, anvils, iron bars, stone mallets, or other simple tools useful in a fight. Kevin was now a hodgepodge of substances, none of which seemed to be normal human flesh and blood, and he was self-conscious about other people seeing him this way. Especially Gwen.

"Oh, gross! What happened to you, Levin?" Albedo said mockingly. "And here I thought you were ugly before!"

"Who asked you?" Kevin swung one stone hammer fist at Albedo, who managed to snatch up a palm-sized Level 4 gadget and activate it in his attacker's direction, causing waves of energy to radiate outward and propel Kevin backward.

"How can Gwen stand to look at you?" Albedo teased, knowing he had struck a nerve.

"What kind of name is Albedo anyway?" Kevin retorted, getting to his feet and charging at Negative Ben with renewed furor. But he was forced back by the invisible waves of the tiny but powerful pulsating alien tech device.

"'Albedo' is a real word, actually," Gwen couldn't help offering. "It's the light reflecting off a planetary body." She fired a pink blast of focused manna energy and hit the offending device square on, blowing it to smithereens. "So Albedo is literally a shadowy reflection of Ben."

"Fascinating," Albedo yawned, setting off a Level 3.5 explosive device and ducking for cover behind the main computer console.

Gwen quickly generated an energy shield over the ticking tech before it went off at her feet. She lost sight of Albedo for a moment, but Kevin caught him as he popped up from the other side of the mainframe.

"How did you get out of jail, anyway?" Kevin asked, genuinely curious, taking another swing at Albedo. As a former criminal himself, Kevin had done his share of time in lockups, including the dreaded prison dimension, the Null Void.

"A benevolent benefactor sprang me out." Albedo grinned slyly, dodging out from under Kevin's crushing blow and throwing a Level 5 plasma grenade Gwen's way.

Gwen's curiosity was piqued. "Anybody we know?" she asked, leaping aside and generating a large magenta dome to protect herself and Kevin from the concentrated explosion of crippling alien energy.

"Doubt it," scoffed Albedo, a little singed from his own explosion. "I'd never met him before, myself. A gentleman by the name of Psyphon." Albedo ripped a Level 6 pyrosphere from its protective casing and slid it across the floor. Everything it passed warped grotesquely in its wake.

Gwen and Kevin tensed at the sound of that name. But they didn't let it slow them down. Gwen quickly conjured a set of energy steps in the air in front of them, and they used them to escape the dangerous pyrosphere on the ground.

Albedo-Ben and his selfish quest to repair his Omnitrix might be the least of their problems, for Psyphon was the right-hand man of the most powerful villain in the galaxy, Ben's number-one nemesis, Vilgax! If Psyphon really was involved in this, then so was Vilgax.

Just then, Albedo surprised them by igniting a Level 3 smart shield in front of him, producing a concentrated flash of piercing white light—an alien tech smoke screen of sorts. By the time Gwen and Kevin could see again, Albedo was gone!

CHAPTER FOUR

Meanwhile, in his prison cell, somewhere in space, greatly outnumbered by monstrous alien creatures, Ben was bracing to defend himself to the death.

"After all I've been through saving the universe time and time again, Ben Tennyson isn't about to go down without a fight!" he cried. "With or without using the Omnitrix!"

Ben heaved his left arm over his head, preparing to use the weighty device on it, the only weapon he had, as a bludgeon. But before he could swing it at his approaching attackers, a very strange thing happened.

The ring of alien creatures around Ben each dropped to one knee and bowed their heads reverently.

"All hail Ben Tennyson! Wielder of the Omnitrix! Savior of the universe!" bellowed an intimidating behemoth that looked like a cross between a reptile and a sloth.

"All hail Ben Tennyson! Wielder of the Omnitrix! Savior of the universe!" recited the rest of the assembled frightening-looking aliens in unison.

Ben was stunned. "Um, thanks?"

This is not at all what he was expecting, and he wasn't entirely sure exactly what to do. "How do you know who I am?"

The creatures continued to kneel in silence.

The reptilian sloth, eyes downcast respectfully, addressed Ben. "You, Ben Tennyson, are famous through-out the galaxy for saving every planet from invasion by the HighBreed. All sentient beings owe you our homes, our lives."

"If anyone can free us from this dungeon, the great Ben 10 can!" the Vulpimancer enthused.

"Can I have your autograph?" the slimy slug asked sheepishly.

Ben lowered his weapon. His overburdened arm was getting awfully heavy anyway.

"Wow. I mean, great! I mean, I sure wish Kevin and Gwen were around to hear you guys saying this, ha ha,"

Ben chuckled, picturing his friends' exasperated expressions. "Er, you may rise."

The creatures all shuffled to their feet.

"I am Clithe of the Reptopithicus," the reptilian sloth alien said.

"How do you all know how to speak English?" Ben asked Clithe.

"I do not understand to what you refer, this English," the creature replied. "How do *you* know how to speak Bagdanarian? And a very specific regional dialect too. Impressive."

"Bagda-what? Oh, of course," realized Ben, slapping his forehead with his free hand. "The Omnitrix works as a universal translator, the way Plumbers' badges do. We're all talking in our own languages, whatever they are, and we're all hearing everyone else translated into whatever language it is we each understand."

"Very useful," the slothlike reptile said, gesturing with its two-toed hand to Ben's wrist.

"Oh, this isn't the Omnitrix," Ben explained. "It's a — well, I don't really know what it is."

He wondered how he was ever going to save these creatures, much less himself, from this place without the use of the Omnitrix. And once this monstrous group realized that Ben 10 couldn't actually come through for them, how much longer would they hail him as their hero? They might decide to retaliate.

"It's a repo boot," his scaly cellmate offered knowingly, inspecting Ben's arm. "Used to deactivate stolen or otherwise sought-after alien tech for easier retrieval by law enforcement officials or other," he paused, "less reputable individuals."

"Like bounty hunters," Ben nodded in recognition, remembering his first encounter with such a device in the hands of the infamous intergalactic repo men, the Vreedle Brothers.

Ben's reptilian cellmate inspected the gadget encasing the Omnitrix.

"I think I can jimmy it," Clithe said thoughtfully. "This is certainly not the first repo boot I've ever removed."

"Because you're a criminal," Ben blurted out without thinking. "That's why you're here in this dungeon. You all are."

Looking at the grizzled alien faces around him, Ben wondered how wise a move it would be of him to help his fellow inmates escape back into society.

"What makes you so sure about that?" challenged the Tetramand.

"Appearances can be deceiving," the slug added.

"You're in here too," the web-footed WildMutt growled. "Does that make *you* a criminal?"

Ben wasn't sure what to think, but he knew that if he was going to be able to help these creatures, he needed their help first. He held out his booted arm to the aliens: "Hack it."

It felt like hours there in the darkness as the reptilian sloth struggled to cross wires and redirect the energy pathways of the repo boot. One of their fellow inmates surprised them all by igniting his own head, Pyronite-style, to produce a little light to work by. It took great effort.

"These restraining collars we've been forced to wear render us unable to use our full powers," the orange-headed creature explained.

Just as Ben was beginning to think cracking the repo boot was a lost cause, Clithe pressed one last button on the electronic device and backed away.

"Wait for it." He grinned.

The repo boot shuddered and fell to the ground! Ben's arm was free! More importantly, so was the Omnitrix.

Ben wasted no time—he immediately started turning the watch's dial, scrolling through his available genoarchetypes. That was Azmuth's fancy term for the Omnitrix's alien forms. The familiar three-dimensional, holographic silhouettes of Brain Storm, Echo Echo, and one of Ben's newest transformations, the magnetic beast, Lodestar, flashed one after the other.

"They look okay," he said, relieved, his face lit from below with the watch's green glow.

Ben's fellow inmates stared at him in awe, gasping at the sight of the one true Omnitrix, the most powerful device in the universe, fabled in song and story.

"Stand back!" commanded Ben. "I'm getting us out of here!"

He dialed the watch to display the most enormous alien of all his selections, one that Ben knew could bust through anything: Waybig!

"Wait." Clithe put a two-pronged hand on Ben's shoulder. "Our captors are not yet aware the Omnitrix has been liberated, yes?"

Ben smiled with comprehension. "Aha, I get what you're saying. Something more low-key so we can sneak out of here undetected."

Clithe nodded. "We'll be long gone before anybody even knows it!"

"It's hero time!" Ben slammed the watch face and called out the name of his most stealthy alien. "This looks like a job for Big Chill!"

A flash of green energy filled the room and engulfed Ben's body. He imagined himself deep inside the Omnitrix, where his DNA would be melded on a molecular level with that of the sampled Necrofriggian.

But when the Omnitrix's transformative power subsided, it was not the incorporeal Big Chill who stood in Ben's place.

"Rath!" bellowed Ben's mightily muscled alien form, flexing his ample bulging body into muscle-man poses and aggressively inviting the confused onlookers to feel his biceps.

Ever since Ben and Kevin had unsuccessfully tried to hack the Omnitrix, it had been acting strangely. Now Ben could never be sure what the Omnitrix was going to turn him into. He had been going for invisibility, quiet, stealth. Instead he got the very opposite! Rath, one of Ben's newest creatures, was a loud, belligerent, 1980s-style wrestler, all sound and fury. Ben couldn't have chosen anything less low-key if he'd tried!

"Let me tell you something, Clithe of the Repto-pithicus," sputtered Rath, getting all up in Clithe's whiskered face. "Rath doesn't know the meaning of the word fear! Rath doesn't know the meaning of the word quit! Rath doesn't know the meaning of a lot of words! But Rath will take on all comers, and he will be victorious!"

"Ben," Clithe interrupted, "with all due respect, this is not what we had in mind. Sneaky, remember? Quiet, remember?"

"Silence!" Rath ranted and raved. "Rath will not be quiet! Even though he just told you to."

In his blur of unchecked rage, Rath seized the restraining collar on Clithe's neck. Its power arched between them painfully, lighting up the chamber with blue sparks!

"Ow," Rath stated succinctly once the electricity had dissipated.

"It's going to take more than brute force to remove these restraining collars. Believe me, we've tried," hollered the Tetramand as he used two of his three arms to heave Rath across the room and his remaining arm to try to keep irritated Clithe from following.

The Tetramand asked the Reptopithicus bluntly, "Are you sure the Omnitrix bearer knows what he's doing? He is just a human, after all."

Rath hit the steel door to the chamber. He got to his feet and turned his seething frustration against the sealed portal.

"Now you listen here, door!" he shouted, pointing an angry finger at the highly fortified panel. Rath didn't care that his enemy was inanimate. It still deserved a verbal smackdown. "Rath will not be denied access to any doorway, anytime, anywhere! Nothing will stand in Rath's way! Not even you, door!"

Rath released the full force of his fury at the immense metal plate. It dented under Rath's repeated punches, then toppled forward with a resounding clang. They were free!

Sirens began to wail. Red emergency lights flashed. Guards were on their way!

"This is not exactly the sneaky, quiet escape I had in mind," Clithe muttered. "We'd better get moving. Fast! Before we're recaptured!"

Rath paused to kneel beside the fallen door, shouting at it triumphantly: "And stay down!"

CHAPTER FIVE

Outside the camouflaged Plumbers' HQ, Albedo-Ben broke the silence of the sleeping city as he bolted from the security elevator and onto the dark, deserted street.

"Suckers," he sniffed. He was constantly surprised at how easy it was to ditch humans like Kevin and Gwen.

He reached into his jacket pocket and pulled out a tiny keychain shaped like a Sumo Slammer character from the real Ben Tennyson's very favorite television series. In all the commotion of the battle below, Albedo had managed to use Ben's own handy little USB drive to steal the Plumbers' top secret intel about the Omnitrix! "Got the file. Now all I have to do is get back to—"

"Going somewhere?" called out a singsong voice.

It was Julie!

Albedo couldn't help laughing in her face. "I'm sorry, but for a second there I thought I was in trouble. What are you doing here? You don't have any powers."

But Julie was not alone. "Here, boy," she whistled.

"*Shiiiip!*" intoned a deep voice with such force that it caused the street and everything on it to vibrate. Albedo's eyes widened as an enormous alien battleship slowly lowered through the cloud cover overhead. Julie's pet Ship had used his Mechomorphic abilities to transform from his default state as a cute, puppy-sized blob into a real spaceship!

With Ship hovering menacingly in the air behind her, Julie glared at the white-haired, red-eyed, red-jacketed Ben.

"Isn't it past your bedtime, *Ben*?" she demanded, her hands on her hips. "I mean *Albedo,* isn't it?"

"Pleased to officially make your acquaintance, my dear," Albedo bowed gallantly. "Now if you will excuse me—"

"Not so fast," Julie warned. She raised her hand in silent command.

In response, Ship's anti-aircraft guns whirled around on his hull and trained their sights on Albedo.

"I wouldn't move if I were you," she stated coldly.

Albedo froze, nervous, but kept his composure. "Fair enough," he stated, raising his hands in surrender. "I throw myself upon your mercy."

With that, he threw himself at Julie! Thanks to her athletic prowess from years of competitive tennis, Julie, though caught by surprise, instinctively dodged his attack.

Ship's computerized sighting system expertly followed the infrared image of Albedo's heat signature, but could not get a clear shot. Albedo kept moving, cleverly keeping Julie between them, knowing Ship would never risk hurting her.

"See, this is the problem with having friends," said Albedo with a superior air, "always having to look out for each other. If your ship friend here didn't care about your safety, he could just shoot us both and be done with it. Problem solved. But friends make you weak. They get in the way of your success." He backed away slowly as he spoke, ready to make his escape.

Suddenly, Albedo found himself fully encased in a magenta energy bubble!

"Hey!" he cried in surprise.

"Yeah, you're right," said Gwen as she and Kevin stepped onto the street. "Having friends close by is never useful."

"Touché," Albedo groused.

A few minutes later, Albedo was locked in energy cuffs onboard Ship. "Ha! Capture me if you will, but I'll never tell you where Ben is."

"We don't need you to," said Gwen with a shrug. She was holding the Sumo Slammer keychain drive they had confiscated from Albedo. Her eyes glowed pink. As she concentrated, the tiny keychain slowly rose into the air above her hand and rotated in space. She was using one of the remarkable Anodite powers she had inherited from her alien grandmother, Verdona, to try to sense her cousin Ben's unique life force wherever it was in the universe. His favorite Sumo Slammer keychain had his manna signature all over it. All Gwen had to do was search for a match.

"Getting anything?" asked Kevin, replacing his ID mask over his face.

"Shh, I'm trying to concentrate," Gwen whispered, closing her eyes.

Kevin made himself comfortable in the pilot seat. "Just tell me the coordinates as soon as you've got them, and I'll punch them into the navi-computer," he said.

Julie climbed into the co-pilot seat beside him. "Ship will be able to take us there in no time. Won't you, boy?"

The Mechomorph's familiar, blobby little head materialized from the matching black and green dashboard and happily chirped in the affirmative, "Ship!"

"Found him!" Gwen announced.

The Sumo Slammer figurine stopped glowing and fell back into her hand. She hurried over to the pilot's console to relay Ben's location to Kevin.

"Looks like we don't need you after all, Albedo," admonished Julie with a tense frown.

Albedo's red eyes twinkled with delight. "Ah, but I have something you do not."

They stared at him blankly. Kevin stifled a laugh. Albedo's duplicate Omnitrix wasn't functional. The files he had stolen from the Plumbers to try and repair it were back in their hands. What could he possibly have that they didn't?

"Ben's ugly face?" joked Kevin.

"Exactly," Albedo replied, grinning back at them.

CHAPTER SiX

T his way!" the face of the real Ben Tennyson cried out as he led his fellow escapees down a dungeon corridor while alarms blared all around them.

They rounded several corners, then skidded to a halt as they came face-to-face with an approaching squadron of saucer-shaped robots! Sensing the life forms in front of them, the floating disks immediately sprouted multiple skinny, metallic appendages, each with a Level 5 blaster at the end.

"Fire!" their computer-generated voices intoned as they advanced on Ben and the other fleeing prisoners.

"Everybody split up!" Ben ordered the menagerie of monstrous creatures following his lead.

Ben dove to the ground just as one of the mechanical enemies' laser blasts pierced the wall behind where his head had been moments before! Crouching on the floor, he rapidly scrolled through the alien holograms on his Omnitrix: Goop, Jet Ray, Upchuck. Ben knew he was going to need some serious muscle on his side against all these attackers.

"Good time to go, Humungousaur!" he called out, his right hand slamming the face of the watch with heroic purpose.

Instantly, Ben was bathed in a spectacular green glow. His flesh, his bones, his very genetic structure were manipulated by the energy of the Omnitrix, transforming his DNA into that of a powerful alien creature.

Powerful but small.

"Echo Echo!" his electronically enhanced voice cried out.

"Aw, man." Echo Echo shook his head, looking down at his short stature. "Either Humungousaur's been on a diet, or the Omnitrix is messing with me again."

Ben had become the tiniest of his currently available alien forms: a little, white, robotic creature called a Sonorosian, with the power to manipulate the force of sound—an amazing ability, to be certain, but hardly the hulking strength that Ben had been going for.

"Omnitrix bearer, look out! On your left!" warned the Tetramand, gesturing urgently with one of his three hands. Several of their hovering, metal adversaries had dropped down beside Echo Echo and began firing at point-blank range!

But they didn't call Ben's alien "Echo Echo" just because of his link to the force of sound. Echo Echo quickly demonstrated another of his significant powers—duplicating himself into two copies. The robots' deadly laser blasts passed harmlessly through the gaping hole Echo Echo left behind.

"There's more to me than meets the eye!" one of the twin Sonorosians began.

"Or more *of* me, we should say," the other finished.

"Good one!" the first Echo Echo congratulated his other self.

The two Echo Echoes high-fived, then turned their attention toward their attackers. Both little Sonorosians opened their mouths and screamed a forceful wave of energy that demolished the robots! Unfortunately, a moment later, more floating mechanical menaces soared in to take their places.

"Think you can outnumber us, eh?" one of the Echo Echoes challenged.

The two Echo Echoes multiplied themselves even further, expanding horizontally like a string of paper dolls unfolding.

"Wall! Of! Sound!" they called out in unison, rushing toward their opponents, mouths agape with invisible waves of audio energy relentlessly pouring out.

Their piercing drone filled the corridor. Even safely out of the direct line of fire, the Tetramand clamped two of his three hands over his ears and used his third to cover the hearing area on the giant slug as the Echo Echoes' painful vibrations buffeted the oncoming robots. Most of the floating mechanisms shuddered and burst into flames. Others fell to the floor in pieces.

"We've got to keep moving!" The Echo Echoes had ceased their noisy attack, but the amphibious Vulpimancer still had to shout this to be heard over the constant barrage of sounding alarms.

"Follow me!" all of the Echo Echoes chirped together, running in all different directions.

"Whoops, sorry," a single Echo Echo said. One by one, each of the other duplicates were pulled toward him, until there was only a single Sonorosian left.

A moment later, he was bathed in the green light of the Omnitrix's energy and had turned back into Ben.

"Over here!" Ben waved at the group to follow him down another corridor.

Elsewhere in the dungeon, dozens more flying attack 'bots were mobilizing, and a growing battalion of Techadons were on the march.

"Omnitrix bearer is escaping. Retrieve Omnitrix bearer," chanted the garrisons of mechanical guards. They had their orders.

Rounding another corner, and another, Ben and his cohorts could now see a thick steel door at the far end of the corridor up ahead of them.

"Ben?" Clithe asked hopefully, running alongside Ben.

"Fingers crossed," Ben answered, pushing up his left sleeve to reveal the Omnitrix. The reptilian sloth crossed the two toes on his hand.

Without breaking stride, Ben dialed and slammed the Omnitrix. In a green flash he continued his forward motion, now rolling instead of running, and announced himself as "Cannonbolt!"

"Yeah!" he shouted. "Thank you, Omnitrix! For once you got it right!"

Cannonbolt was a stocky, armored, armadillolike alien of the Arburian Pelarota species, who could roll into an impenetrable ball to bowl over his enemies. Or, say, plow through a dungeon door.

"Out of my way!" Cannonbolt cried, barreling faster and faster toward the heavy metal barrier.

With an excruciating crunch, Cannonbolt blasted a massive, gaping hole right through the door!

"We're free!" Clithe led the group in cheering.

Cannonbolt stood up outside, no longer in sphere form, and peeked back through the opening he'd created.

"Come on!" he called back to his fellow inmates.

The aliens raced toward the door and freedom. Before they could all make their escape, however, a Techadon stepped around the corner into the far end of the corridor behind them. Its mechanical wrist whirred open, revealing an enormous repeating photon blaster. It took aim at the fleeing inmates and fired mercilessly! The aliens scattered, running for their lives, as the guard's laser blasts exploded all around.

"I'm hit!" Clithe cried out in pain, falling to his knees, his scaly hide smoldering from the blast.

"Hang on!" Cannonbolt spun into action. He rolled back inside the prison to help his new friend. "Everybody else out! Move!"

Bolting for the exit, the Tetramand, the froggy Vulpimancer, the snail, and the whole gang looked back over their shoulders — or whatever they had instead of shoulders — watching with respect and admiration as Ben, who could have very easily continued on with them to freedom, roared back into harm's way to come to the aid of someone he barely even knew.

"That's why he's a hero," the slug said with a proud sniff.

The liberated alien inmates burst out of the dungeon and into the daylight. The Tetramand squinted his four eyes and looked up. There was a spectacular palace perched high above! Their dungeon, its passages, and all its prison cells had been carved into the rock underneath.

Back on the other side of the dungeon door, Cannonbolt bounded toward the Techadon with a vengeance.

"Fry, my friend, will you?" bellowed Cannonbolt.

The Techadon responded by firing more laser blasts, searing a swath of destruction hot on the heels of the zig-zagging Cannonbolt. Ben's spherical creature gathered momentum, then zoomed his way up the far wall and across the ceiling directly over the Techadon! The robot's deadly photon rays continued to follow Cannonbolt, tearing a jagged, continuous trench in its target's wake, including through the solid stone over its own head!

"Not too smart, are you?" Cannonbolt observed.

Massive chunks of stone ceiling that had been loosened by the Techadon's blasts crumbled down onto the robot, denting its shoulders and knocking it off balance. But, true to its programming, the Techadon kept its gun sights trained on the enemy: Cannonbolt.

Off to the side, Clithe coughed and struggled to drag himself clear of the growing destruction. His charred gray snakeskin was painfully seared and cracked, and he winced from the effort.

Taking advantage of the Techadon's laser blasts tracing his every move, Cannonbolt raced up, down, and all around the walls, ceiling, and floor of the prison corridor, drawing the Techadon's fire wherever he went.

"Nyah nyah! Can't catch me!" he taunted his pursuer.

Satisfied with the extent of his handiwork, Cannonbolt skidded to a halt beside the prostrate Clithe and unfurled himself into an upright position.

"One thing I've learned battling any kind of single-minded robots," Cannonbolt lectured, "is to use your enemy's power against him. Check it out."

Clithe fought to lift his head and watched as the compromised structure of the entire corridor around and above the Techadon collapsed in an avalanche of stone and steel, pummeling the battlebot into an unrecognizable heap of twisted metal. A moment later, it was buried under the mass of debris it had created!

When the dust settled, the reptilian sloth alien smiled weakly.

"Thank you, Ben Tennyson," Clithe breathed, barely above a whisper. "You truly are a hero."

Cannonbolt powered down into Ben and knelt near the injured alien.

"We've got to get you out of here before more of them show up." Ben could already hear the whirring and clanking of reinforcements on their way. "Come on!"

But the injured Reptopithicus creature had stopped moving.

"Clithe?" Ben gingerly shook the creature's shoulder, but there was no reaction.

Ben bowed his head in silent respect for his fallen friend, then stood up to make his exit alone.

Suddenly, Clithe's body shuddered once, twice, and as Ben looked on in horrified fascination, the creature's entire layer of damaged skin sloughed off in one continuous piece!

"Ew! I did not need to see that," Ben said queasily.

'm all right, Ben Tennyson." Clithe's hoarse voice took Ben completely by surprise.

"You're alive?" Ben could not believe it, not after what he'd just seen.

The reptilian sloth stood up and stretched, revealing an unblemished layer of brand-new flesh! His old, charred, snakeskin shell lay empty on the ground at his feet, looking like his lifeless, gray double.

"That," started Ben quietly, then burst into feverish excitement, "was the coolest thing I've ever seen! How'd you do that?"

"We Reptopithici always shed our skin as soon as we outgrow it," Clithe said nonchalantly, "or otherwise have the need. I am sorry if I alarmed you."

"Pffft!" Ben batted his hand in the air. "I wasn't worried. Much."

"Must retrieve the Omnitrix!" a robotic voice boomed down the corridors.

"*Now* I'm worried," Ben added grimly. His right hand reached for the watch on his other wrist.

Several other electronically processed voices were chiming in. "The Omnitrix bearer has escaped! Find him! Bring him back for our Master!"

A half dozen enormous, armored Techadons, flanked by a swarm of the smaller, aerial battlebots, came clamoring down the corridor toward the breached dungeon entryway. Their sensors registered the existence of Clithe's restraining collar nearby and zeroed in on the reptilian sloth.

"There's one of the inmates that escaped with the Omnitrix bearer!" a Techadon bellowed.

"Seize him! He will know where the Omnitrix is," added another mechanical guard.

"Take him to our Master," a third electronic voice intoned.

"The Master will force him to lead us to the Omnitrix bearer for retrieval," another Techadon agreed.

Hidden for the moment behind Clithe's bulk, Ben had a sudden idea. Instead of dialing the Omnitrix and transforming for another battle, Ben quickly slipped inside Clithe's discarded, burned snakeskin.

"There's a second one, sir!" a Techadon intoned as it trained its massive arm blaster on a gray Reptopithicus clumsily getting to its feet beside the first.

Ben, in disguise, raised his reptilian sloth–like hands in surrender.

"What are you doing, Ben Tennyson?" Clithe asked urgently.

"Sh," Ben whispered back to him. "They want to take us to their leader? We're going to let them!"

"Kraaaack!"

A sonic boom thundered across the sky as space-ship Ship broke the sound barrier passing through the atmosphere.

"Ship!" the Galvanic Mechomorph's deep voice announced.

"We're here," Julie translated.

On board, Kevin leaned back in the pilot seat with his feet up on the console. Julie sat beside him in the copilot seat. Gwen stood behind Kevin's chair, and their prisoner, Albedo, lurked in the background, energy cuffs still sizzling with power around his wrists. They all watched the viewscreen intently as the cloud formations parted and revealed their destination below.

"There!" Gwen pointed to a peak on the craggy, gray landscape. It was an ominous-looking royal palace overlooking a vast alien city. She had traced Ben's manna signature halfway across the galaxy to this very spot.

"Take us down, please, Ship," Julie directed her pet politely.

Ship descended and soared in a graceful arc around to the back of the fortress. From this vantage point, the passengers noticed a flurry of activity at the base of the mountain under the palace.

"Hold up!" Gwen cried with alarm.

On the ground far below, a legion of heavily armed, flying robots was searching the surrounding landscape, while several enormous Techadons marched in formation, single file, out of a mutilated steel door in the rock face.

"Hm, big doings in the castle dungeon," Kevin observed. "Looks like Tennyson already got himself out of there. He must be someplace outside on this planet now. We'd better go pick him up before—"

"No," Gwen said, her fingertips at her temples in concentration. "He's still inside. Somewhere. I'm sure of it."

"Then let's do this thing," Kevin stated. He gestured at Albedo. "Uncuff him."

Gwen leaned over the back of Kevin's chair and whispered in his ear, "I know Albedo's unarmed, but there's no way we can possibly trust that guy."

"I wouldn't trust Albedo any farther than I could throw him. Uh, than *Julie* could throw him," Kevin clarified. "No offense."

"None taken," Julie replied.

"But I know how criminals think," Kevin continued. "And Albedo's working some angle here. We've got to find out what it is. And how Psyphon is involved, since we know for a fact that Psyphon is the righthand man of . . . "

"Vilgax," Psyphon's voice finished.

In the cavernous throne room of the palace above the dungeon, surrounded by the alien-medieval decor of looming statues on pillars and ornate tapestries depicting the pillage and plunder of many a conquered world, the scrawny, sycophantic alien known as Psyphon bowed humbly before the throne of his formidable liege, the most terrible villain the galaxy had ever known: Vilgax!

"What do you mean the Omnitrix is no longer secure in my dungeon?" Vilgax bellowed in fury, towering over his cowering toady. "Curse that Ben Tennyson!"

Vilgax's imposing presence was further enhanced by his intimidating, armored physique and hideous, ten-tacled features. He had tangled with that annoying Earth brat, Ben Tennyson, many times before, both as a ten-year-old child and now as a teenager. And without fail, every time, that pathetic little excuse for a hero had somehow managed to defeat Vilgax, the great and pow-erful (self-proclaimed) destined ruler of the universe and rightful wielder of the Omnitrix!

But soon that would all change. For this time, Vilgax had procured himself a skilled accomplice, duped into doing his dirty work for him—a creature even more desperate for access to the Omnitrix than he, and willing to do anything, or go through anybody, to possess it.

"Every Techadon on Vilgaxia has been deployed to retrieve Ben Tennyson, sire," Psyphon stated as con-fidently as he could. He was used to dealing with his boss's fits of rage, but that didn't make his job any easier.

"The Omnitrix will not get far. By the time Albedo returns with the necessary Plumbers' information, Ben Tennyson will have been returned to captivity."

"And once the true Omnitrix has served its purpose," growled Vilgax, "Ben Tennyson will no longer be needed."

"That was brilliant of you to order me to break Albedo out of jail, oh wise and powerful Vilgax." Psyphon knew how to lay the compliments on thick.

"That annoying Galvan Albedo is the only other being in the universe who ever even got close to duplicating Azmuth's creation," hissed Vilgax conspiratorially. "Who better to have build me my own working Omnitrix?"

"By making him believe you are helping him build it for his own use as well," Psyphon added gleefully. "So he can change himself from his current hideous human form back into his normal hideous Galvan form."

"Of course, how was I to know the little white-haired brainiac wouldn't be able to power the new copy he built without linking it through the real Omnitrix," mused Vilgax.

Unbeknownst to Vilgax and almost everyone else, there was much more to the operation of the Omnitrix than there seemed to be. Most aliens and people assumed that the Omnitrix itself stored an abundance of alien DNA inside of it. In actuality, the watch was like a wireless device communicating across the universe with a massive mainframe that really housed its database of DNA. Under the shroud of secrecy, the Galvan had built an entire planet called Primus specifically designed to be a one-of-a-kind, organic machine, whose neon-green lava flows contained the DNA of every sentient species in the universe! Large, mechanical mosquitoes known as Apis Metalifera came and went constantly from the volcano on Primus like honey bees to a hive, depositing their collected DNA samples in bursts of energy into the flowing green lava. The Omnitrix worked only by communicating with this hidden planet-wide database.

This was the true secret of the Omnitrix. Without access to any off-site DNA, the Omnitrix was just a fancy-looking bracelet and nothing more. Like the nonfunctional one Albedo currently had decorating his own wrist.

"Patience, master," said Psyphon soothingly. "Very soon your hard work and dedication all these years will pay off, and you can retire to the glory of universal domination that you so rightfully deserve. With me at your side, of course," added Vilgax's sidekick with a grin.

"I've heard enough!" a voice shouted.

Psyphon and his master whipped around as Ben Tennyson burst into the throne room!

"Vilgax!" Ben pointed accusingly. "I should have known you were behind this!"

"Ah, Ben Tennyson." Vilgax grinned triumphantly. "How gracious of you to save me the time and effort of hunting you down." He took a threatening step toward Ben.

"I wouldn't do that if I were you," warned Ben, his right hand hovering over the Omnitrix.

They faced off tensely for a moment.

Vilgax towered over Ben, but Ben could not be intimidated. The adversaries locked eyes, each silently daring the other to make the first move.

Psyphon erupted into nervous giggles, gleefully rubbing his palms together. "The suspense is killing me!"

CHAPTER EiGHT

Permission to enter, Master Vilgax," a robotic voice intoned.

Before either Ben or Vilgax budged, the silence of their standoff was broken by the hydraulic whirring sounds of a hulking Techadon noisily entering the chamber, escorting the two recently recaptured reptilian escapees.

"These two inmates were accompanying the Omnitrix bearer when he escaped," the Techadon droned. "They may have information on the current whereabouts of Ben 10."

"You bucket of bolts for brains." Psyphon pointed to the teenaged boy locked in a tense standoff with Vilgax. "Ben 10 is right here!"

"Vilgax!" cried the shorter, grayer of the two Reptopithici, stepping forward. Then this alien shocked everyone in the throne room by tearing off his entire outer layer of skin and revealing the real Ben Tennyson hidden inside!

"Albedo?" Vilgax shouted in surprise at the newcomer. He assumed the real Ben Tennyson was already standing before him. "Why are you sneaking around like that, confusing the Techadons?"

"And what did you do to your hair?" Psyphon added, noting that this Ben sported a brown 'do as well.

Vilgax turned and scowled back at the very same face still next to him. "Albedo's return marks the end of your usefulness to me, Ben Tennyson. Don't bother to struggle. You're completely surrounded. All we require is the energy of the Omnitrix. Surrender it now, and I may just spare your life."

"Yeah," the Ben closest to Vilgax pretended to ponder the offer. Then he added formally, "I think not!"

He hit the dirt suddenly as a ray of magenta energy blasted out from the shadows of the palace vestibule, shattering an elaborate bas-relief above the throne and knocking Vilgax out of the way.

"Ben?" Gwen called out. She raced into the chamber

and spotted the duplicate across the throne room. She glanced back and forth between the identical-looking Albedo-Ben and Ben.

"Gwen!" the real Ben shouted happily. "Boy, am I glad to see you here! How'd you guys find me?"

"Er, well, it actually didn't take us too long to get here," Gwen explained sheepishly, "once Julie helped us realize Albedo wasn't you."

Ben crossed his arms, irritated. "What? Oh, thanks a lot, guys, for *finally* noticing I was gone! And what was Albedo doing hanging out with Julie anyway?"

"Can we save the chitchat for later, people?" Kevin yelled. He appeared behind Gwen, morphing his fists into two giant, steel hammers as he ran.

"Kevin, where's your ID mask?" Ben asked.

"Here!" The Ben on the floor beside the throne pulled the ID mask off his own face, causing a flash of energy to dissipate and reveal his white hair, red eyes, and red jacket!

"How dare you, Galvan! Double cross me, will you?" Vilgax roared at Albedo, grabbing him by his Omnitrix arm and lifting him off the ground with one hand.

"Well, he *is* a double," Kevin offered, clobbering

Vilgax with a hammer-fisted blow. "What? Somebody had to say it."

As Vilgax sailed backward into a pillar, he released Ben's white-haired twin from his iron grip. Albedo fell roughly to the floor.

"Don't just stand there, Omnitrix bearer," cried the terrified Albedo, frantically crawling behind the shelter of the royal throne. "Make with the Omnitrix bearing!"

"Don't tell me what to do, Albedo," Ben called back, scrolling quickly through the Omnitrix's holographic menu items. "Whose side are you on, anyway?"

"My own," Albedo admitted honestly.

"Do you know these people?" Clithe whispered to Ben, confused as to who was on their side.

"Uh-huh." Ben nodded. "They're my friends. All except the one who looks like me. Come on, Omnitrix," Ben begged, "don't let me down." Then he called out: "It's hero time!"

Ben slammed the face of his watch and disappeared in an explosion of green light. Instantly, his human DNA melded with that of his chosen alien form. When the blinding green energy of the Omnitrix finally dissipated, the creature left standing in Ben's place grandly announced its name.

"Lodestar!"

This strange being, with its head floating as a separate element above its body, was one of Ben's newest alien forms, and Ben was still getting the hang of using it. Lodestar had super powers related to magnetism, which were about to come in handy. Because the towering Techadon behind him was aiming its gun across the room at Kevin!

"Kevin!" Gwen blasted a pink energy shield around Kevin. Her shield cracked dangerously under the pressure of the Techadon's blow, but it managed to hold fast.

"Tennyson! Take care of that Techadon, will you? We've got our hands full dealing with *your* mortal enemy over here!" Kevin yelled, winding up and punching groggy Vilgax with his other hammer fist. "You're welcome, by the way," he added sarcastically.

"Thank you, by the way," Lodestar replied, matching Kevin's sarcasm.

While Kevin and Gwen kept Vilgax busy, Lodestar shoved Clithe to safety. "Get behind me!"

Ben focused Lodestar's magnetic powers on the Techadon. Waves of energy pummeled the giant robot at close range. It lurched forward but did not collapse.

Instead, the Techadon moved to retaliate against its attacker, shoulder cannons rotating into lock-and-load positions!

"It's resisting! It's too strong!" Clithe warned Lodestar.

The Techadon's heavy weaponry took aim at Lodestar.

"Wait for it," Lodestar replied.

The Techadon began to shudder as Lodestar's magnetic fields took hold of all its metal components, internal and external, large and small. Suddenly, the invisible forces under Lodestar's control tore the metal Techadon to pieces!

"Out of my way!" Vilgax growled, slamming Kevin aside with one wave of his mighty arm. "You merely caught me by surprise. You won't be so lucky again."

"Oof," groaned Kevin as he hit the far wall. "I don't know about that. I'm a pretty lucky guy. Ask anyone."

Vilgax climbed up and stood on top of his throne, where he unsheathed the powerful flaming sword he had recently acquired on his planetary tour of domination, during which he had won both the weaponry and the entire worlds of every champion he conquered in battle! He had always been a formidable foe for Ben, but with his newly enhanced weapons and abilities, Vilgax was nearly unstoppable these days. He pointed the sword across the throne room and fired a spectacular blast of energy at Lodestar.

"Oh!" Lodestar groaned in pain, knocked to the ground by the tremendous force of the blow.

"Ben!" Clithe called out to his friend. He clawed viciously at the electronic restraining collar that was preventing him from using his own powers to assist Ben and his friends in battle. He was rewarded for his efforts with a searing electric shock. Clithe growled in frustration. The only way to stop the collar's disruptive influence would be to disengage it at the source. This was the throne room—it had to be around here somewhere! Clithe started searching frantically.

"Give me the Omnitrix and be done with it, Tennyson!" bellowed Vilgax.

Pulling out another one of his recent acquisitions, Vilgax took aim with the powerful Ruby of Rouleau and fired a piercing red beam across the chamber room at the already compromised Lodestar.

"Oh, no you don't!" Gwen grunted as she created a ball of manna in the air and hurled it at Vilgax, sealing him and his attack inside.

The interior wall of the energy sphere took the full

force of the ruby's blast, splintering like an eggshell right in front of Vilgax's face. Vilgax clenched his fist and punched it through the cracked energy ball, sending fragments of manna slicing through the air in all directions.

"Whoa!" Gwen had to duck to avoid being skewered by shards of her own making.

Kevin rushed in and held a giant hammer fist over Gwen like an umbrella. "We can't keep this up much longer," Kevin worried. "With all those new toys, Vilgax is just too powerful for us."

"I'm open to suggestions," Gwen answered.

"Yeah, I got nothing," Kevin replied. "I was hoping you did."

Elsewhere in the throne room, Clithe was exploring the walls, looking for the device that would deactivate his restraining collar.

"Looking for something?" Psyphon held up a piece of alien tech and waggled it at Clithe.

"The master control!" Clithe yelled, leaping at Psyphon.

But the scrawny assistant casually pressed a button on the contraption, causing a jolt of electricity to course through Clithe's restraining collar. Its wearer writhed in agony.

"Ah!" cried Clithe, grasping at his neck.

Psyphon grinned evilly at his victim's pain.

Across the chamber, Lodestar used his magnetic powers to lift up the substantial throne and heave it at Vilgax!

"Being king is a heavy burden," quipped Lodestar, as Vilgax was pinned under the crushing weight of his own throne. "And I do mean heavy."

"Thataway, Tennyson!" Kevin cheered.

Albedo, who had been crouched behind the throne, squealed and scampered away to find a new hiding place.

Lodestar sailed across the chamber and stood triumphantly over Vilgax. "What was that about me surrendering and maybe you would spare my life? Oh, wait, now it's the other way around!" Lodestar taunted Vilgax.

But Vilgax was not that easily defeated. He drew a deep breath and exhaled with such force that the heavy throne shot up off his chest and bashed into Lodestar!

"I grow tired of these games, Ben Tennyson. I will take the Omnitrix now!" Vilgax commanded, rising to his full height. "The Omnitrix or your life!"

CHAPTER NINE

As Vilgax advanced on the fallen Lodestar, Gwen and Kevin rushed at Vilgax from two different directions.

"You hit 'im high, I'll hit 'im low!" yelled Kevin.

Gwen ran up a series of plates of glowing pink energy, which appeared before her in the air like steps. But Vilgax turned toward Gwen, firing laser beams from his eyes that traced every move she made! It was all Gwen could do to use her powers to defend herself. She had no time to counterattack. Another one of Vilgax's ill-gotten powers was getting the best of them!

Kevin transformed his hammer hands into even larger iron anvils and swung them at Vilgax. But Vilgax simply blasted Kevin away with his super breath.

"Losers!" Psyphon cackled, turning away from his own skirmish to mock Vilgax's failing combatants.

Clithe took this split-second opportunity to tackle Psyphon! They struggled, and before Psyphon could knock Clithe back with a punishing electric jolt to the throat, the desperate Reptopithicus wrenched the restraining collar controller out of Psyphon's clutches!

Clithe speared the device with a sharp claw, causing it to spark and erupt in flames. The lights on the metallic ring around Clithe's neck buzzed and flickered, then winked out. He was free! And so were his fellow inmates, wherever they were.

"This is for sending Techadons to take me from my family and imprison me here just so Vilgax could lay claim to my land!" Clithe pointed and snapped his two mighty claws together, creating a resonant shock wave that sent Psyphon flailing helplessly through the air.

"I'm sure that was just a misunderstanding!" the scrawny sidekick howled as he tumbled out of the throne room.

Vilgax ignored his defeated lackey and glared at Lodestar. "You can never stop me from pursuing the Omnitrix, Ben Tennyson. If you manage to escape, I will hunt you down. I will follow the Omnitrix to the ends of the universe, never resting until its power is mine!"

Lodestar stood his ground. "Then I'd better make sure you're stuck here for a while."

Lodestar focused all his magnetic powers at Vilgax, or more specifically, at Vilgax's signature shell of armor. The metal-clad villain immediately began rising up into the air!

"What is this magic?" Vilgax bellowed, unable to twist free from the unseen restraints floating him toward the ceiling. His arms, his legs, his face, every part with any metal armor on it was locked in the invisible grip of Lodestar's magnetic manipulation!

"You might want to reconsider that metal suit of yours," Lodestar said casually as Vilgax continued to rise.

"Some might call it a fashion don't," Gwen chimed in.

"Mmmm!" Vilgax mumbled furiously as Lodestar pinned his tentacled face to the ceiling!

Outside the palace, Psyphon landed on the ground with a thud. He got up and dusted himself off, attempting to regain his dignity.

"At least I'm out of harm's way," he muttered to himself.

"Not so fast," a voice threatened.

It was Julie! Ship was beside her, back in his little blob form, along with a hulking web-footed Vulpimancer, a giant, slimy slug creature, an intimidating three-armed Tetramand, and a host of other former alien inmates.

"You're Vilgax's guy," said one of the brutal-looking aliens, cracking his knuckles, "the one with the Techadons who ripped us from our homes so Vilgax could abscond with our stuff!"

They advanced menacingly on Psyphon.

"Can't we talk about this for a minute?" Vilgax's right-hand man pleaded as the mob backed him toward the palace entrance.

"Get him!" the mob hollered.

"Ahhh!" Psyphon screamed, running back inside the throne room. "I'd rather take my chances in here, where there aren't so many of you!"

But the angry mob pursued Psyphon right into the throne room.

"Clithe!" the Tetramand cried, recognizing their former cellmate. "You're here? Whatever became of the Omnitrix bearer?"

"Here he is," the amphibious Vulpimancer called out, nudging Albedo-Ben from his hiding place, convinced by the Omnitrix on his wrist. "He must be scared though. Look, his hair's turned white!"

"Why does everyone make such a big deal about the hair?" pouted Albedo.

"That's an imposter," Clithe explained to his crowd.

"An Omnitrix bearer wannabe," teased Kevin.

Lodestar stepped up to address the monstrous mob. "What are you all doing back here? Why didn't you just keep running away?"

"When our restraining collars switched off," the oversized snail said, "we knew something must be happening. And we were finally free to be of assistance to you in a fight."

"We couldn't just leave you trapped if you'd been recaptured," another alien acknowledged.

"After all you'd done for us." The three-armed Tetramand bowed his head.

Lodestar powered down into Ben and grinned. "I've got just the job for you guys."

Without Lodestar's magnetism holding Vilgax to the ceiling, the villain came crashing painfully to the floor.

"What'd you do that for, Tennyson?" asked Kevin suspiciously. "You already saw we can't fight Vilgax that easily by ourselves."

"We don't have to," Ben answered, gesturing toward the growing mob of angry former inmates, now with full access to their formidable alien abilities.

With a whoosh, one alien's body ignited into flame. Another alien's claws began whirring like saw blades. Yet another grew to three times its height. The super-powered group with a score to settle closed in menacingly on Vilgax.

"No amount of allies can save you, Ben Tennyson!" Vilgax called out between efforts to defend himself from the crowd of attackers. "This is not over between us! The power of the Omnitrix will be mine one day! Do you hear me? Mine!" Vilgax's threat echoed out of the palace and across all of Vilgaxia.

Outside the castle, Ben, Gwen, and Kevin met up with Julie and prepared to leave Vilgaxia far behind. Albedo stood silently, among them but not really one of them.

Kevin slipped on his ID mask again. "Better?" he asked Gwen self-consciously.

"Eh, you could use a haircut," Gwen kidded Kevin, chucking him good-naturedly on the shoulder. Kevin's appearance meant much more to him than it did to Gwen.

"Ship! Ship!" Julie's pet chirped lightly.

They all watched as Ship transformed himself from a cute little blob into their impressive interplanetary ride.

"*Shiiip!*" announced his booming baritone.

"All aboard," Julie translated.

Ben stood before Albedo, facing his opposite. "I can't believe you actually double-crossed Vilgax to help Gwen and Kevin rescue me." Ben offered his right hand in a gesture of friendship. Astonishingly, Albedo took it!

As the two Bens shook hands, Ben continued cautiously, "I can't help but wonder what's in it for you."

"Why, double-crossing *you* of course!" Albedo quickly grabbed Ben's left hand with his own free left hand, clamping their Omnitrixes together!

Before Ben could react, the power of his, the one true Omnitrix, linked to Albedo's dud, and lightning arced spectacularly between them!

"Ah!" cried Ben, more in surprise than in shock from the electricity.

Gwen, Kevin, and Julie were knocked off their feet by the concussive force of the Omnitrixes meeting. Glowing green energy irradiated both Bens.

"I think it's working!" Albedo gushed, his red eyes gleaming. "Something's happening!"

There was a sudden flash of green light of such intensity that it drove Ben to his knees. And just like that, Albedo was gone!

In his place now stood a tiny, gray, bug-eyed alien creature. A Galvan! It blinked up at Ben.

"He did it!" Ben exhaled, appalled. "Albedo repaired his Omnitrix with mine and turned himself back into a Galvan!"

CHAPTER TEN

I cannot believe you would mistake me for Albedo!" the Galvan standing before them griped. "I'm clearly more handsome than he ever was." He crossed his skinny, little alien arms in irritation. "Oh, so all we Galvan look alike to you, is that it?"

"Azmuth?" Ben recognized the touchy personality of his mentor.

"Yes, it's Azmuth," the tiny gray alien groused. "And I see that once again you cannot be trusted with my Omnitrix!"

"What happened to Albedo?" asked Ben curiously. "He disintegrated!"

"You wouldn't know disintegrated if it walked right

up and blasted you into a million pieces," Azmuth grumped. "*That* is not what disintegration looks like. I teleported the greedy little nuisance out of here and into a holding cell on Galvan to await trial for his growing list of crimes. We Galvan are tough, but we're fair. He'll probably only get a thousand years or so. Give or take a century."

"So Albedo didn't fix his Omnitrix?" Ben breathed a sigh of relief.

"Luckily for you," harrumphed Azmuth.

"What about those top secret Plumbers' files on the Omnitrix that Albedo stole?" asked Kevin, holding up Ben's Sumo Slammer keychain drive.

"Fakes," the Galvan stated. "Decoys planted with the aid of the Plumbers to throw would-be Omnitrix hackers off the track."

At the mention of hacking the Omnitrix, Kevin and Ben shifted uncomfortably.

Azmuth continued, "The Omnitrix is far too complex a device for a mind like Vilgax's to comprehend. Albedo, however, now *he* had a real shot at cracking it. But then, he had the best teacher in the galaxy."

"Too bad about him being all evil and everything," Kevin said.

"Indeed." Azmuth nodded wistfully. Then he hopped up onto Ben's wrist and tapped the watch.

"Wielding the Omnitrix is a grave responsibility, Ben," Azmuth admonished his charge.

"I know," Ben agreed.

"But I believe the Omnitrix chose you for a reason," Azmuth continued.

"I know," Ben nodded.

"And so despite your many, many flaws," Azmuth added, "I have great faith in you to continue to fulfill your heroic destiny."

"I know," Ben repeated.

"Stop saying 'I know.' You're getting on my nerves, kid," Azmuth complained.

"I know," said Ben, smiling.

Back on Earth, it was early evening in Bellwood when spaceship Ship appeared in the darkening sky and came in for a graceful landing on the outskirts of town. The gangplank slowly lowered, and Ben and his friends disembarked. As soon as they were on solid ground, the enormous spacecraft collapsed into a little black-and-green blob that fell in line behind them.

"Ship! Ship!" it yelped.

Julie turned around, crouched, and patted her pet on the head. Or on what would have been Ship's head if he'd had one.

"Who's up for a celebratory Mr. Smoothy?" she asked, rubbing her hands together in anticipation. "Peanut butter seaweed, Ben? On me?"

Ben's stomach growled. "Man, I don't know how long it's been since I've eaten anything," he complained, rubbing his empty belly. "I sure could go for a double order of chili–cheese fries."

Kevin, Julie, and Gwen froze in their tracks. They all shared the same terrifying thought.

"Albedo!"

Gwen spun around, punched her clenched fists out in front of her, and blasted Ben with a powerful manna ray. She locked him in her energy, scanning his life force to confirm his true identity.

"Ow! Hey! What'd you do that for?" Ben gasped in surprise, waving his hands in front of his face in a futile effort to make it stop. "If you'd rather get burgers instead, just say so!"

Gwen powered down, releasing him.

"Sorry. Just checking."

Chapter Book #3
The Dark of Knight

Turn the page for an
exclusive sneak peek at the
next Ben 10 Alien Force
chapter book!

CHAPTER ONE

O n your left, Tennyson!"

Kevin Levin's cool, raspy voice echoed over the deafening barrage of laser fire coming at him from every direction.

At night, warehouses by the shady docks in any city would be considered dangerous. But the current attack was way above and beyond what any normal town would expect. Then again, Bellwood was hardly a normal town.

"Ha!" Kevin leaped through the air, grunting with effort. As he did, his fist grew, stretched, and morphed into a giant boulder. With a resounding *gong*, it struck the knight in shining armor that was charging at his friend.

The Forever Knight—as these medieval-looking villains were known—wobbled in place for a moment. He held his helmeted head as his whole body vibrated like a bell, then collapsed to the ground in a clanging heap.

"I saw him, Kevin! Chill, will you?" Big Chill called back in his usual breathy voice.

The thin, blue, bug-eyed alien unfurled his hooded cloak into a pair of bisected wings and zoomed straight up into the air as two more Forever Knights tried to close in on him from either side.

A member of the alien species known as a Necrofriggian ("necro" meaning death and "frigid" meaning extremely cold) native to a subzero planet called Kylmyys, Big Chill was so named by Ben because he had the mysterious ability to freeze objects with his breath or touch—and that is precisely what the creature did now. Hovering above his would-be attackers, Big Chill exhaled a gust of freezing wind on the Knights, covering their armor in a sheet of ice that pinned their arms to their sides and their feet to the ground.

"Forsooth!" exclaimed one of the Knights in surprise as he toppled over. The other's teeth were too busy chattering to say anything.

"Hold it right there, you two," breathed Big Chill. "I mean, *freeze*! Heh heh."

Every time Ben took this particular alien form, he couldn't seem to resist making puns that referenced the low temperature.

"Cool it with the cold jokes, will you, Ben?" Gwen Tennyson sighed at her cousin. She was busy using her own alien-enhanced abilities to generate powerful magenta shields of pure energy to protect herself from the zigzagging red blasts that tore through the air. The remaining Forever Knights had not slowed down the attack with their deadly laser lances.

"Heh. You said 'cool it,'" chuckled Big Chill, his cloud of icy breath visible in the still night air.

"Why did you turn into Big Chill anyway, Ben?" asked Kevin with more than a hint of irritation. He was struggling to fight off some Forever Knights in hand-to-hand combat. Or in Kevin's case, hand-to-giant-rock-fist combat. "I mean, come on!" he continued. "The Forever Knights wear armor, dude. That's metal. Lodestar could've taken these guys out with one, uh, magnet tied behind his back!"

"Don't you think I tried to turn into Lodestar, Kevin?" asked Big Chill, making himself intangible just in time to allow several laser blasts to pass harmlessly through him.

"Do I look like I care?" Kevin growled at Big Chill, hammering Forever Knights out of his way with his huge metallic fists.

"You're the one who asked," Big Chill breathed back, equally irritated with Kevin. Ben knew perfectly well that if the Omnitrix had just turned him into Lodestar, like he'd wanted, this fight would have been over almost immediately. He didn't need Kevin to rub it in.

"What are these Forever Knights doing anyway?" Gwen's voice rang out above the din of the laser fire as she blasted Forever Knights with magenta energy beams.

"What are they always doing?" Kevin barked. "Probably stealing alien tech. Duh!"

"I know the Forever Knights are usually at the docks trying to steal alien tech," Gwen retorted huffily. "What I meant was, what are they doing with *that*?"

Two of the remaining Forever Knights were trying to sneak away with a wooden crate. Gwen lassoed them with a ropelike beam made of manna and jerked the heavily armored bad guys together, crushing the wooden box between them into splinters! The Knights struggled helplessly, bound by Gwen's powerful energy stream, as a strange alien artifact fell to the ground at their feet.

"And don't 'duh' me," Gwen finished, turning to glare at Kevin.

"Sorry," Kevin apologized.

"Allow me," Big Chill breathed in his creepy voice, swooping in to grab the piece of alien handiwork. His semitransparent, ghostlike self passed right through the cluster of Knights, but Big Chill had to make himself tangible to pick up the object from the ground.

"Ah!" Big Chill cried out as soon as his fingers made contact with the strange alien artifact. A blinding flash of green light engulfed him, forcibly transforming him back into Ben Tennyson!

Ben crumpled to the ground with a groan.

CHAPTER TWO

Ben!" cried Gwen, rushing to her cousin's side.

Kevin swung around and batted away the remaining Forever Knights with the huge iron ball that was his fist.

"What happened?" murmured Ben groggily. One second he had been Big Chill, the next he was his regular human self, all without ever activating the Omnitrix. That was not the way the watch usually worked.

"Must have been that alien artifact," Gwen said, pointing to the mysterious object on the ground beside Ben. She moved to pick it up herself. If it was powerful enough to affect Ben like that even with the Omnitrix, they'd better not leave the thing lying around.

"Ah!" she shrieked, dropping the piece of strange material like a hot potato. "It burns!"

In response to Gwen's contact with the device, all of her magenta energy still lingering on the scene instantly dissolved. As her manna lasso faded away from around the restrained group of Forever Knights, they took the opportunity to escape.

"Run away! Run away!" they cried in their British accents.

Kevin rushed to Gwen's side. "You okay?" he asked.

"I-I think so," she stammered, rubbing her hand where it had touched the device.

"It must be some kind of energy conduit," added Ben, shaking his head to clear it. He got to his feet. "Never seen anything like it before."

"Wonder if my old running buddy Argit could get a good price on it for me on the black market," mused Kevin. Kevin and his untrustworthy alien pal Argit had been involved in many a shady business dealing together in the past, including boosting Grandpa Max's old camper, the Rustbucket. Argit and Kevin had conspired to sell off the myriad of alien tech with which the Rustbucket was tricked out. That plan had not gone very well for Kevin. He still didn't like talking about it.

Kevin noticed that Ben and Gwen were staring at him with displeasure. "I meant 'we.' Maybe *we* could get a good price for it. I was going to share with you guys," Kevin covered.

"Uh-huh," Ben frowned, somewhat suspiciously. After all the adventures they'd been through together, Ben had grown to trust Kevin, often with his own life. But occasionally there were little moments like these, when Kevin would let a hint of his old self slip out. Ben couldn't help but wonder if their so-called "friend" Kevin wasn't always a hundred-percent reliable.

"Stand back," Ben said. "This could get ugly."

He took off his long-sleeved green jacket with white racing stripes and a black and white "10" and wadded it up over his hand protectively as he reached for the alien artifact.

"Ugly's my middle name now," said Kevin, brushing Ben's cloth-covered hand aside.

"I thought your middle name was 'Ethan,'" smiled Gwen. Then added, elbowing him in a good-natured teasing way, "'Kevin E. Levin.' Somebody's parents had a sense of humor." She giggled.

"Right, *Gwen*. And *Ben*. And what's your brother's name again, Gwen? Oh, that's right: *Ken*!" Kevin smirked back. "I'm just surprised Grandpa Max's name isn't *Glen*."

"Now, now, kids," said Ben, stepping in between his friends like a referee. "Don't make me separate you two."

"Seriously, though," Kevin interjected, the smile dropping from his face. "I think I've heard of this kind of alien tech. But I never believed it was real."

Kevin squinted down at the piece. At first glance, it appeared to be a generic hunk of rock, but upon closer inspection, it was revealed to be a foreign metallic compound of a sort not found on Earth. Etched into its surface were strange markings, alien glyphs, which the well-traveled Kevin now strained to decipher.

"Can you make out what it says?" Gwen asked him.

Kevin had surprised his friends several times in the past with his ability to read alien languages. For a guy without much formal schooling, Kevin was actually pretty knowledgeable — especially about matters of alien significance.

But as he studied the particular alien object before him now, Kevin frowned and tipped his head to the side. "It's only got pieces of letters on it, I think, no whole words," he said.

The alien artifact had jagged edges. It looked as if it had been chipped off a much larger object, almost like a single piece of a larger puzzle.

"Whatever it is, we'd better not leave it here," Ben said grimly. "It's obviously pretty powerful, and the Forever Knights are bound to come back for it."

Ben reached for the artifact again with his protectively padded hand, but Kevin intercepted the move with his own inhuman palm.

"You've both got energy powers," Kevin said, nodding toward Ben and Gwen. "I don't. Not anymore." He hung his head in sadness for just a moment, then looked up. "Let me have a crack at it."

Ben and Gwen stood by tensely, prepared to intervene at a moment's notice if necessary to rescue their friend from any ill effects of the artifact. After what it had done to each of them, who knew what it might do to Kevin?

Kevin wiggled his fingers in the air above the piece, hesitated for a beat, then grabbed it.

Everybody winced in anticipation. But nothing happened.

"Huh," Kevin grunted, surprised and a little disappointed.

"Must have used up all its power on us," Ben ventured a guess.

"Maybe," added Gwen, not at all convinced.

"I wonder what the Forever Knights were going to do with it?" Ben thought aloud.

"Doesn't matter now." Kevin tossed the seemingly inert artifact up in the air a couple of times with satisfaction. "Finders keepers. Losers," he paused, then shrugged, "losers."